# Anno's Britain

## MITSUMASA ANNO

PHILOMEL BOOKS
NEW YORK

## OTHER BOOKS
## BY MITSUMASA ANNO

*Published by Philomel Books:*

Anno's Magical ABC:
An Anamorphic Alphabet

Anno's Animals

Anno's Journey

Anno's Italy

Anno's Medieval World

The King's Flower

The Unique World of Mitsumasa Anno:
Selected Works (1968–1977)

First USA edition 1982.
Published by Philomel Books, a division of
The Putnam Publishing Group, 200 Madison Ave., New York, N.Y. 10016.
Originally published in 1981 by Fukuinkan Shoten Publishers, Tokyo,
as *Anno's Journey III* by Mitsumasa Anno, copyright © 1981 by Kuso-kobo.
All rights reserved. Printed in Japan.
Library of Congress Cataloging in Publication Data
Anno, Mitsumasa, 1926–
Anno's Britain.
Summary: The illustrations lead the reader on a
journey through Great Britain moving freely through time
and space.
[1. Stories without words. 2. Great Britain—
Pictorial works] I. Title.
PZ7.A5875Ab 1982   [Fic]   81-21058
ISBN 0-399-20861-5   AACR2

In the past few years Mitsumasa Anno has made a number of long journeys, traveling far from his native Japan to see at first hand Europe's art and architecture and to study its music and its languages, its people and its literature. With sketchbook and camera in hand, he wandered at leisure, observing and recording what he saw along the way from his own unique perspective. He has distilled these experiences into two other "Journey" books, ANNO'S JOURNEY (northern Europe) and ANNO'S ITALY, which express in pictures the impact each place makes on the traveler as he moves across the landscape. He sees people working, playing, living; he sees them in quiet country villages or large, bustling cities. Without a word of text, Anno fills each page with life, conveying to the observer his joy of discovery and recognition.

This third "Journey" takes Anno to Britain, the "mainland" Britain of England, Scotland and Wales. Anno has visited there before, but this is a special journey, a journey mainly in praise of Britain's countryside. He explains how it came about: "On one of my visits to London I discovered a book in which there was a map of Britain that was unlike any I had seen before. Instead of the large towns being prominently marked, it was the small, charming villages that were featured, with the towns shown just as dots. As well as this fascinating map, the book gave details of village work, of thatching roofs, of spinning wool and of shoeing horses. I was so intrigued that I was determined to see these places and activities for myself, and, inspired by the book, I traveled from village to village. The people I met take great pride in their villages, and will protect them against change, particularly against

their growing into large cities. They love their countryside and love living there, caring for their surroundings. I discovered that the villages of Britain are the most beautiful in the world."

And as Anno's lone traveler journeys through the countryside on horseback he encounters a wealth of detail that will delight the viewer: scenes from Shakespeare's *Romeo and Juliet*, *Hamlet*, *The Merchant of Venice*, *King Lear*, and *A Midsummer Night's Dream*; characters from beloved British books: Doctor Dolittle, Winnie-the-Pooh, Mary Poppins, Alice, Peter Pan, the Happy Prince, Peter Rabbit, children from Kate Greenaway's illustrations and from Mother Goose rhymes, as well as Dick Turpin, Sherlock Holmes, Robin Hood and others. There are activities such as the Oxford and Cambridge Boat Race, cricket, and bagpipe playing; there are idyllic pastoral landscapes from paintings by Constable and Gainsborough, and much, much more.

But Anno did not altogether turn away from the towns and cities of Britain. You can find the traveler in the book in Winchester, Canterbury and Windsor, and of course he journeys through London, where he sees famous landmarks like St. Paul's Cathedral, the Tower of London, and Big Ben—and where more than once he passes the Queen taking one of her dogs for a walk. Anno is as intrigued by the Royal Family as are all observers of Britain. "I had almost finished this picturebook when I saw the television broadcast of the Royal Wedding on July 29, 1981. It was so beautiful I decided to add it as an historical note.

"This book is dedicated to the British people and their villages."

## About the Artist

MITSUMASA ANNO is known all around the world for his beautiful and imaginative picturebooks, designed for children but appreciated and enjoyed by adults as well. Winner in 1977 of the Golden Apple Award of the BIB (Bratislava International Biennale), he has also received the Boston Globe-Horn Book Award, the Brooklyn Museum of Art/Brooklyn Public Library citation, and many other awards and honors.

Born in 1926 in Tsuwano, a small historic town in the western part of Japan, the artist was graduated from the Yamaguchi Teacher Training College and was an art teacher for a time, before deciding to devote himself entirely to his writing and painting. In addition to the visual arts, his widespread interests include architecture, history, geography, mathematics, science and literature, and have led him to travel widely. His breadth of culture and his evident enjoyment of the beauties and wonders of our world enrich every one of his books, and their readers as well.